LOVESTORIES&OTHER
LOVESTORIES&OTHER
LOVESTORIES&OTHER
LOVESTORIES&OTHER
LOVESTORIES&OTHER
LOVESTORIES&OTHER
LOVESTORIES&OTHER
LOVESTORIES&OTHER
LOVESTORIES&OTHER
LOVESTORIES&OTHER
LOVESTORIES&OTHER
LOVESTORIES&OTHER
LOVESTORIES&OTHER
LOVESTORIES&OTHER
LOVESTORIES&OTHER

LOVESTORIES&OTHE
LOVESTORIES&OTHE
LOVESTORIES&OTHE
LOVESTORIES&OTHE
LOVESTORIES&OTHE
LOVESTORIES&OTHE
LOVESTORIES&OTHE
LOVESTORIES&OTHE
LOVESTORIES&OTHE
LOVESTORIES&OTHE
LOVESTORIES&OTHE
LOVESTORIES&OTHE
LOVESTORIES&OTHE
LOVESTORIES&OTHE
LOVESTORIES&OTHE
LOVESTORIES&OTHE

Love Stories & Other Love Stories

Published by Long Day Press
Chicago, Il 60647
LongDayPress.com
@LongDayPress

ISBN 9781950987115 (Paperback Edition)
ISBN 9781950987146 (eBook Edition)

Library of Congress Control Number: 2021930002

Edited by Joseph Demes
Designed by Joshua Bohnsack

Acknowledgements:
Versions of the following stories have been previously published in *Smokelong Quarterly*, *Cosmonauts Avenue*, *Passages North*, Amazon's *Day One*, *Hobart After Dark*, and *Gigantic Sequins*.

Printed in the United States of America
First Edition

Love Stories & Other Love Stories

JUSTIN BROUCKAERT

Long Day Press
Chicago

"A book like a trip through a cartoon amusement park—fun, fast, colorful, strange, bouncy, bendy, and exhilarating."

—Ben Loory, author of *Tales of Falling and Flying*

"Justin Brouckaert writes of a Michigan and Midwest I know well: a mixture of kindness, silence, and a place where truly anything can happen. What resonated with me reading this collection is how Brouckaert is thinking deeply about what it means to belong (be it as a misplaced astronaut, a C+ husband, a hill among hills) and even more crucially, how we understand that a place, a moment, a person is the right thing to make a part of our identity."

—Megan Giddings, author of *Lakewood*

"Justin Brouckaert's *Love Stories* is full of smart, witty tales, uncanny marvels that never once failed to surprise me. I read these stories with a smile plastered on my face and, often, a small skip of uncanny terror in my heart—and I couldn't ask for a better combination."

—Matt Bell, author of *Appleseed*

Contents

This Is What I Know About Being Gigantic

after Minus the Bear

When you're gigantic, no one appreciates your dancing. They doubt your coordination. They're all so worried about their tiny little skulls.

When you're gigantic, you lose respect for the trees. There's just no reason to be in awe of what's smaller than you. Even the tiny people underfoot are only worth watching when they blend together in droves & sway blue & white like the rolling waves of the ocean look when you wade in the middle of it, water up to your thighs, the cold prickle of coral breaking skin between your toes. Or when they flicker so green you want to lie down on your back & thrash in them like a puppy in a perfect field. The tiny people don't like it when you do this. They tell you to stop in angry ways. They shout *earthquake* or *meteor* or *why, God? Why?*

When you're gigantic, it's hard to make friends, even with the one tiny person who has settled on your ankle. Every day he learns a little more about his home, and you, still growing, learn a little less about his body. One day the tiny settler is discovered. The ankle-land is annexed. First there are ten tiny people & then there are a hundred & they begin to climb. You feel your tiny settler protest, his tiny body swaying, but he is outnumbered. You imagine he looks up at you in apology, but at your size it's hard to discern such features. The tiny colonists multiply, give birth to whole families on your calf, dig deep in your thighs with their fingers & toes, climbing higher & higher until they threaten to topple you, to bring their gigantic home crashing down.

When you're gigantic, the speed of your growth surprises you. Suddenly you can't feel the sharp bodies digging into muscle, the pinpricks on your skin. You can't see the tiny people pointing & it hurts your neck to try. The oceans become buckets for your feet. Your swinging arm strobes the sun. One day none of this is true & the next day it is.

When you're gigantic, you have lots of time to think about how gigantic you are. Once a tiny little person with a tiny little nose, you're now an eclipse, brief & forgotten. There was a rush that came with size, new size, an unmatched feeling of power & dominion, but that allure is fleeting. Instead, what lingers is the thought of how unrecognizable you've become, how indistinct & mountainous. How the tiny people must stare & stare but really see nothing.

When you're gigantic, you never stop growing. Everything you've ever known becomes a molecule & everything you've ever been is sky. You are bigger than sky. Your head pokes out the earth's atmosphere & you gasp for air to fill those gigantic lungs. Your neck breaks through to the starry black & shoulders & arms quickly follow. Comets & asteroids shoot past like bullets, clipping your earlobes and fingertips, making great craters in your gigantic nose. You are picked apart, made smaller this way, shot at again & again until, like everything gigantic, you eventually crash.

When you're gigantic, it's hard to keep things in perspective. It's easy to forget there's no one to catch you, that the tiny lights witnessing your collapse are not fireflies but stars. The clouds, a cool breeze on your back. This is what I know about being gigantic: you never really forget what it's like to be small. Even in the end, you are between one size & another.

When you're gigantic, the crash happens slowly. Tiny people live & die. They look at you like you're forever. When you do come down, you don't come down easy. There is dust & fire & lost religion, everything broken & bloodied around you. When the detritus clears, when your gigantic body is grounded & burnt by stars, the tiny people come with their tiny fists in the air. They are organized & efficient. They have been waiting. It is best to close your eyes.

The Men Who Flew Away

There is no welcome party waiting for the three men from Earth when they touch down on the planet they have been traveling so long to reach. They are greeted instead by a vacant asphalt lot cracked with weeds, penned by a square of battered buildings—a far cry from the landing zone filled with revelers they were told would anticipate their arrival.

The three men step down from their ship onto alien land. They walk across the alien lot and down an alien street until they meet their first alien.

You there, says the first man. Are you part of the delegation?

The delegation? asks the alien.

We're ambassadors of peace, says the second man. From Earth.

Listen, buddy, I don't know what you're talking about, says the alien. It pulls a hood over its head and walks away.

The three men explore the new planet together. They find a cluster of buildings near the landing site, the sky-scraping structures not unlike the ones they knew back home. They strap their survival packs tight around their waists and venture cautiously into the heart of it.

The first two men walk guardedly, each keeping a hand on his pistol, but the third man begins to notice that this alien city doesn't look so dangerous after all.

He sees a red–and–white storefront similar to the pharmacy where he'd gotten his prescriptions filled. He spots a squat building with a black awning that looks just like a restaurant where he and his wife had dined on Sunday afternoons. His eyes linger on a two-story structure identical to the bar all three men had visited together after their final training session at the space station, sharing one last pitcher of beer before rocketing from earth.

The crosswalk symbols show a blue man walking and a bright red hand. A police car blasts by, sirens blaring. A few aliens stare at the men in their spacesuits. Most just keep on walking.

This doesn't seem so alien, the third man thinks. This doesn't seem so strange.

The other two men stop at the window of a building that reminds the third man of his favorite fast-food restaurant. They all peer through the window, through their reflections, at the aliens eating inside.

Funny, says the third man cautiously, how it looks so much like home.

The first man probes the wall of the building, bringing his eye to the brick to measure its slant.

Something's not right, he says.

Like what, says the third man. What exactly?

I don't know, says the first man. Something, though. I can feel it.

The second man presses his face to the window, staring hard at the blue–and–orange–striped wallpaper wrapped around the room.

Something's definitely not right, he says. Something is definitely very wrong.

When the three men approach what appears to be a grocery store with a newspaper stand out front, the third man stops the others.

There, he says. The trio ventures cautiously toward the building and forms a huddle around the primitive machine.

The date on the paper is the same date as indicated on their wristwatches.

The cities in the paper are the same cities they came from.

The newspaper is the same newspaper they read every day on Earth.

Up to this point, it had been a terrible, gnawing suspicion. But now he's sure of it.

We've made a mistake, the third man says. We got lost and landed right back where we started.

It's a trap, say the others. An alien trap! They pull their pistols from their belts and survey the street for danger.

The third man urges them to wait, but already the other two men are backing away, pistols cocked at their chins, leading the retreat back to the ship.

The third man protests while the other two men prepare the vessel for departure.

I know this city, he says. I know that street.

They're tricks, says the first man. Alien tricks!

They're shapeshifters, says the second man. They've shapeshifted the whole damn place.

The three men had heard stories of hostile alien encounters, but their superiors had believed this planet to be peaceful. The men were not trained for war.

Even if this *was* a different planet, says the third man, some alien planet, there's not enough fuel to make it back home.

There will be enough, says the first man. There has to be enough.

Those shifty fucks! yells the second man. He spits, suddenly wracked with anger and disgust. Those hideous monsters!

But they look just like us, says the third man.

No, says, the second man. No, I'd rather die out in space than at the hands of those freaks.

The third man tries to argue, but his companions have already taken their seats in the cockpit.

We can't risk any more time here, says the first man. Are you coming or not?

The third man has spent countless hours with these men in training and in travel. He's learned to trust them with his life—but he also trusts his own intuition. He's called this city home for much longer than the other two, who only relocated when training began. There is no other city that lights up like this city, that stings with salty air and thunders and rumbles beneath his feet like this city. From his very first step off the ship, the man felt in his bones the familiar thrum of home.

While the other two men turn to the controls, the

third man slips down the stairs, leaving his survival pack and his pistol. He locks the hatch shut above him and jogs from the ship as its engines glow red and roar to life. He stands at the edge of the lot until the heat from takeoff slowly leaves his cheeks and the ship soars above the star-scraping buildings, above the iconic skyline, up and away.

The abrupt departure of the man's companions leaves him uneasy, but he grows more comfortable as he walks the familiar path toward home. The man has been sequestered in his spaceship for years, nothing but sterile white within and endless darkness without. A deep sense of relief settles over him as he spots familiar landmarks, once part of his daily commute: his café, his market, his park along the water.

The city is almost exactly as the man remembers it. Occasionally he finds himself searching for a once-familiar building now boarded up or razed, the lot entirely transformed, or wanting to turn down a street he doesn't quite recognize. In these moments the man reminds himself of how long it's been since he's walked this city.

It's only reasonable, he thinks, that these small changes—and lapses of memory—should happen over time.

The man takes the subway to his station and walks the three blocks to his apartment, arriving home at his building as the sun rises. He enters, walks down the hall and stands in front of his door, his heart beating faster than when the ship first left earth, when he was shot into zero gravity for the very first time. The man takes a deep breath, and knocks.

A robed woman answers holding a mug of coffee. When she sees the man at the door, she drops the mug. It shatters between them.

The woman bursts into tears and throws her arms around him.

It's you, she says. It's really, really you.

The man and his wife waste no time contacting the agency that organized his voyage. Later that morning, they meet with the new commissioner—more tears and disbelief.

We thought you were lost, says the new commissioner. Do you remember the connection cutting out? The static?

No, says the man. I guess I don't remember that at all.

He's had a tough time of it, says the woman.

He has, indeed, says the new commissioner.

I'm just happy to have him back, she says.

As are we, says the new commissioner. In fact, the entire country will be overjoyed.

Oh, says the man. Will they really care, you think?

Of course they will, son. The new commissioner grips the man's shoulder. You're our returning hero.

By the end of the morning, the man has done interviews with local radio and the TV news. The coverage is picked up by all the national programs, and soon he's seen on every cable station and heard across the airwaves. His face is stretched and squinched to fit every computer monitor and phone screen.

The mayor organizes a city-wide parade for that afternoon, honoring the man as grand marshal. He rides with his wife at the end of the procession. They wave dumbly to the thousands of people who line the streets.

At the end of the parade is a podium, and the man is asked to give a speech.

I don't really know what to say, he says when he's ushered onstage. I've never given a speech before.

Speech, speech! the people chant.

I'm happy to be home, the man says, but I guess I'm just not so sure I deserve all this.

You do, you do! the people chant.

We set out from here years ago with a mission, he says. And we failed. We failed everyone.

You did what you had to do, the people chant. You came back home!

The men who flew away might seem foolish or crazy, says the man, but they were the ones who led me here safely. If I were as brave as they were, I could have kept them from leaving. If I were brave, they would be here today.

The man puts his hands on the sides of the podium and begins to cry.

It's me, he says. I'm the one who left them behind.

After a few moments of silence, the new commissioner touches the man's shoulder and escorts him offstage.

The man's debriefing with the new commissioner doesn't last long.

He set out with the other two men as ambassadors of Earth to a newly discovered planet. Each man brought gifts to deliver to the planet's leaders, who were believed to be friendly. They were to dine with the planet's dignitaries, expressing Earth's desire for a mutually beneficial partnership. The men weren't agents or spies; they had no ulterior motives. Their pistols were only for their protection.

Some time during those years of travel the men lost radio contact with earth. The voices they thought were their superiors were really echoes of previous correspondences, calls of *Roger* and *Copy* and *Go* the men had praised for their efficiency.

The ship followed the coordinates programmed into the mainframe. There was an error, and the ship looped back around while the men were sleeping. Coordinates were swapped, or there was a warp, a shift in the fabric of space. Somehow, the ship mistook home for their foreign destination. Unknowingly, the men rocketed back toward earth.

The agency is sweeping space for the men who flew away, says the new commissioner. As of right now, we've found nothing.

What about the dignitaries? asks the man. Were there repercussions for our failure?

The new commissioner shakes his head.

I'm afraid, he says, they no longer accept our calls.

The next two weeks are a whirlwind. Though he and his wife hoped to spend time reconnecting after the parade and the debriefing, the man is whisked from talk show to talk show, to speaking engagements across the country. He is asked to comment on the future of space travel, of intergalactic relations, the atrocities taking place on nearby planets—issues for which he has no answers. He is asked to share secrets, to predict the future, to rewrite the past.

If you could say anything to the men who flew away, the people ask, what would you say?

Well, the man responds, I'd say I hope they found their way somehow. He imagines the men desperate, their reserves depleting. He imagines their shock at landing on a nearby planet to refuel and realizing their error. Or worse: years later, landing at their now-unfriendly destination.

I don't think we've heard the last of them, he says. I think that some day they'll be here to speak for themselves.

At night, the man sleeps in hotels the agency has booked for him.

At the end of a long day of speaking, of shaking hands and smiling for pictures and signing auto-graphs, he comes back to his room and locks the door behind him. He begins his ritual of lifting each item from its place, holding it up to the light and turning it, examining its sides. On one of his first nights on the road, the man came back to his room and was convinced his door and his frame were not aligned. Or if not the door then the hallway, and if not the hallway then the pattern on the carpet, and if not the pattern of the carpet then the pattern on the wallpaper that seemed in some way blemished, scrambled, immeasurably shifted in a way the man couldn't quite name. He found himself circling the building, running his hands along the walls until dawn.

The man tries to push away thoughts of his crewmates, of the difference they couldn't articulate at the fast-food restaurant, the thing they felt—more than they saw—was wrong. The ritual becomes a compulsion: he examines the telephone, the nightstand drawers and the books inside. He examines the lamp and all of the towels and soaps and lotions. He slides his hand along every sheet on his bed, the pillowcases and the headboard.

When he's finished, the man is frustrated and queasy and tired. He pulls his mattress from its frame and positions it in front of the sliding door leading out to the balcony. Thousands of miles away, his wife waits for him to return to his half of their bed after an unbearably long absence. For now, he draws the curtains from the window and falls asleep with the stars.

When the man finally arrives home, his wife sits on the living room sofa and watches him probe their belongings, running his hands over them and under and around.

This picture, he says, holding an old photograph of the two of them.

Yes?

Was this—

Our first anniversary, she says. Fifteen years ago, almost to the day.

I'm sorry, the man says. He sits down and holds his head in his hands. It's just so hard.

Don't be sorry, his wife says. You've been through a lot.

Yes, he says. I guess I have.

At night the man and the woman get into bed together. They talk for some time. They make love, slowly and timidly. Afterward, the man stares at the ceiling.

What are you thinking? the woman asks.

Oh, nothing, says the man.

He suddenly feels tired, more tired than he has felt in a long time, his weeks of travel finally taking their toll. The woman rests her head on the man's chest. He fights sleep for a while—there is still so much more to examine, walls he hasn't traced—but his eyelids start to flicker until the room goes gray, until the walls warp and shudder and eventually fade. The woman waits until she feels the man's chest rise and fall evenly, until his breath becomes steady. She presses her hands flat to his naked body and smoothes his skin with her hands from his neck to his ankles, and when she's sure he's asleep, she slips herself inside.

The Grand-mothers

The grandmothers walk through the front door, two and three at a time, bonding over talk of the weather. They lower their umbrellas, brush raindrops from their shawls and smooth their sheen gray hair, propped up in helmets or draped over grandmotherly shoulders. *Cats and dogs*, they say. *Absolutely cats and dogs.*

A few of us are sent to herd the grandmothers toward the macaroni artwork, but they can't be corralled. One begins reorganizing the library; another labels science lab beakers in size 20 font. The grandmothers test the locks on classroom doors, pull tacks from hallway corkboards. Ricky Cunningham's grandmother gently lectures the pregnant secretary on the merits of cloth diapers while Brianna Mack's grandmother slips and sprains her ankle on the bathroom floor. We sympathize with Brianna Mack's clumsiness—such a sweet girl, and quiet, too—but when Eunice Mack cries out in pain, those of us leading students down the hallway feign deafness. *Eyes forward*, we command. We increase our pace.

A handful of grandmothers walk into the kindergarten wing and, within seconds, disappear. We send Ms. Bellweather to the intercom like a sentry to the alarm.

The grandmothers have arrived, she says, her voice atremble. *Students, please locate your grandmothers.*

Do we blame Principal Schultz? Do we think him a

fool for not learning from the great Father/Son Spaghetti Lunch Disaster of 2011, the Family Fitness Night Revolt of 2009, the Community Roof Repair Calamity of the early aughts? Would we think poorly of any man so eager to show off minor cafeteria renovations? Had we tried bribing certain weaker members of the board to veto this dreadful event? Impossible to say, really. There are so many of us, and we rarely assemble.

Ms. Lopez smiles politely as one grandmother interrupts her history lesson to teach students proper cursive. Through a clenched jaw, Ms. Womack thanks the grandmother who's picked the lock on her classroom door to give her desk a thorough dusting. Principal Schultz, he's not such a terrible man. Better, at least, than the others. But we are not through with him, not yet.

In the cafeteria, nervous grandmothers wander from the snack line to the hot lunch line, back to the snack line again. Fussy grandmothers brush their grandchildren's hair, button their buttons, tie their shoes. *Are you hungry?* the fussy grandmothers ask. *No*, the grandchildren say. *Are you sure?* the fussy grandmothers insist.

When the children roll spitballs, when they dump salad on their shoes, when they use their fingers as rubber band guns, the grandmothers turn their heads. We teachers swoop in to scold.

We teachers, we have our complaints. Do we ask for much? Just crayons and books and tissues, occasionally an ousting. And it's true: we don't let our students down. We are, after years on the job, hardwired for discipline and care. But we teachers, we feel insulted. Principal

Schultz thinks us insurance for the grandmothers' negligence.

The grandmothers wander back to the kitchen. In minutes, they've churned out trays of cookies and brownies, sugary treats the students jump out of their seats to inhale. A few teachers, the same ones as always, are ready to threaten mutiny. The rest of us pray for strength.

At the end of lunch, Principal Schultz begins his speech. On behalf of *Crestfield Elementary*, he starts, but his voice is quickly overpowered by the grandmothers' applause. They sidle up to him and pinch his cheeks, slide their hands down his jacketed arm. *Beautiful speech*, the grandmothers say. They ogle and pry. *Gray already?*

We collect our students and lead them to safety.

We are open to forgiveness until we see our classrooms—our sanctuaries, our zones of control—rendered unrecognizable: educational posters replaced with floral print and hummingbirds, glass knick knacks on the shelves where books should be. Clusters of desks separated and padded with cushions, plastic chairs made into rockers, a podium swallowed by violet crochet work. Hours of summer organization, ruined; each chamber of learning transformed, in minutes, into a grandmother's den. They've left us notes of admonishment, critiques of our design. *A perfectly suitable space*, the notes say. *The years will teach you.*

We teachers, we are furious. Our spaces have been violated. Our computers are locked from excessive login attempts.

We leave our students with *Magic School Bus* reruns

and track the grandmothers by the sticky hard candies left in their wake, the perfumed breeze of old receipts that linger in the air like pollen. We find them outside the music room, dancing to an orchestra of squawking recorders. It's Principal Schultz we want, but he's collapsed on the floor, weeping, a beaten man, and it makes us even angrier to know they've done our job for us.

Two grandmothers twirl on the tile around him. The rest of them link arms and sway.

Thank you for inviting us, the lead grandmother says, pulling Principal Schultz up from the floor. *We've all had such a wonderful time.* She is wearing hummingbird earrings, a violet flowered blouse. Principal Schultz tries to speak, but the grandmother puts a finger to his lips and turns to the others. She pulls a tuner from her purse, and the grandmothers match pitch. *A-one, and a-two, and a-three.*

Their voices rise in harmony, strong in unison, perfected by years of church choir. Soulful tones, fragile bodies. We teachers, we listen, and in this moment we can't help but admire the coordination of their attack, their skillful pursuit of power. Though none of us will later admit it, we are grateful for this moment of peace they bring us, the perfect stillness of their chorus, the likes of which had never graced our halls before. We listen carefully, but cannot make out the words. The grandmothers are too beautiful, too wise and gentle and sad. We are reverent. Many of us shed tears before we set ourselves upon them.

The Midwestern Man

The Midwestern Man leaves the Midwest. He's thought about it for a long time. *I was born to be alone*, he tells his wife. He jumps on his horse. *Alone with my horse.*

The Midwestern Man rides through Indiana & Illinois. He makes camp in Iowa on a starry night. *I ride alone*, he tells a broken fencepost. The next morning, he repairs it.

The Midwestern Man is caught in a sudden, blinding snowstorm. *A test of fortitude*, he thinks. In his tent, he clutches his hand-carved Al Kaline figurine to his chest & prays for strength.

The Midwestern Man rides south. *Where ya from?* a Texan asks. *North*, says the Midwestern Man. He offers his hand: a good Midwestern hand, dirt beneath the fingernails. *Way up dere*, he says.

A deer wanders a Texan street & the Midwestern Man shoots it dead. *Gotdamn*, says the Texan. The Midwestern Man slings the carcass over his shoulder. He & the horse & the deer head West.

In the desert, the Midwestern Man eats beans between prickly cacti, watches tumbleweed roll. *Hot dog*, says the Midwestern Man. *Just like a John Wayne western.*

In New Mexico, he thinks of his wife. Her busy crochet hooks, her looping tennis serve.
Him on his Lay-Z-Boy with his paper. Her perched on the arm, sighing over his shoulder at the news.

A pang hits him, stronger than hunger. Guilt.
Ope, thinks the Midwestern Man. But he must press on.

In Arizona, the Midwestern Man's horse dies of thirst. The Midwestern Man licks his own dry lips.
Ah, geez, he thinks. He pulls his ball cap tight to his head & takes the desert by foot.

Finally the Midwestern Man sees the ocean. He walks right up to the pier & leans over its edge.
Oh, fuck, he says, looking out at the blue horizon, the tall, crashing waves. *This thing is huge.*

Are you seeing this? he says as he turns to his side.
But there's no one else there beside him.

Later, the Midwestern Man's pen hovers over a postcard bound for home.
I miss you, he thinks of writing.

He wipes his brow & sips a cold-pressed juice. In the distance, a surfer howls.
Weather's fine, he scribbles & drops the note in the mail.

The Midwestern Man makes some friends. *Nice beard,* they say. *Thankee,* he replies.
Dude, they say, *have you ever had Chipotle?* They hand him a burrito. *Holy shit,* he says.

The Midwestern Man makes camp on the beach. At night, he empties his knapsack.
An apple, a comb, a soft block of wood. Pa's old mitt. He sniffs the worn leather & sighs.

The Midwestern Man's friends find more friends & they all sit around a campfire.
I miss crab cakes, says a Man from the East Coast. *You just can't find good crab cakes around here.*

I miss cicadas, says a Southern Woman. *They helped me sleep.*
Everyone turns to the Midwestern Man. He bows his head & runs his hand through his beard.

Already, he misses the thick wool afghan near the woodstove, his wife's body curled into his.
The murmur of summer thunder. Nodding heads & pursed lips at the counter of the general store.

He misses flat land & late-fall snowstorms. The long, hollow scrape of a shovel on a wooden porch. The Midwestern Man looks up. All his new friends are staring. He clears his throat.

There are only three differences between the West and the Midwest, says the Midwestern Man. Everyone leans in to listen. *Location is one of them*, he says. *Winter is the other two.*

The Midwestern Man sweats through the rest of the West Coast summer. He carves wooden figurines & sells them on the boardwalk.

⸘

That one's Fred Flintstone, he says to a fast-walking woman. *And that one's my old dog, Red. Weird*, she says. She stops & flips her hair & adjusts her bag. *What kind of accent is that?*

The Midwestern Man quickly tires of the city. After all, the city is not what he came for. He packs his knapsack & borrows a truck, traveling up the state, then over.

He hikes majestic mountain ranges, hunts secluded forests. He fishes dazzling waters, forages for berries & fruit.

It's all so wonderful—the land is beautiful like nothing he's seen before.
Except for one thing, the most important thing: it isn't *his*.

The Midwestern Man feels like a stranger in the Western wilderness—an invader sometimes.
Park rangers track him through protected forests. Crows eye him with skepticism from the trees.

So, time & time again, the Midwestern Man goes back to the city, the boardwalk, his friends.
Before he knows it, he's been out west two years, then three.

The Man from the East Coast packs his things.
The Midwestern Man clutches his hand. *Say hi for me,* he begs.

The Midwestern Man really starts to think.
One day, it stops him dead in his tracks. *Why did I ever leave?* he wonders.

The idea just up & came to him one day, as far as he can remember.
At the time, he hadn't really thought about it much at all.

These past few years, he's been so decided. But now?
The Midwestern Man *likes* the Midwest. He misses it. He's grown tired of avocados & Sriracha.

How could he have left the woods he walked & whittled? The blasted critters in his yard?
Euchre tournaments! Church festivals! Prep football on crisp autumn nights!

In the Midwest, he'd been surrounded. But without his wife, his land, his people?
It's an ache, the Midwestern Man realizes. He presses his hand to his chest. An actual ache.

The Midwestern Man begins to scheme. He will burst into his home & take his wife in his arms.
Or he will stop at the door, push it slowly open, pull an extravagant gift from his knapsack.

Or he will take off his cap & stand with his hands behind his back. *Nice horse*, she'll say.
He'll look behind him, then back to her. Offer a sheepish grin.

Or she will see him in town, before he rounds the bluff overlooking the lake.
Why I never, she'll say after a long, long silence. Or: *You've got some nerve.*

He misses her—he misses the way her eyes spoke before her mouth.
He misses finding her at her piano, not playing but just letting her fingers tickle the keys.

He misses her 'round the buff, where they'd sometimes walk on late-summer evenings.
He misses her in the lake, on the open water, where her laughter rang for miles.

The Midwestern Man sighs. None of his plans will work.
His wife is a good Midwestern Woman, stubborn as she is strong.

Why leave? Stay! his new friends beg when he tells them. *You're like family now!*
They are beautiful, he realizes, & moreso together—blond & lithe & soft, West Coast bronzed.

They wrap their arms around each other with tears in their eyes.
What will you do without us? they ask.

Ain't nothing personal, says the Midwestern Man. *Just realized I don't belong.*
They flip their hair & brush sand from their arms. *But dude,* they say. *You're, like, totally vital.*

Right, he says. *Listen. I came all the way out here because I was looking for something. But this place has done something to me. I think I've changed.*

But dude, his friends say. *Don't you see? It's what you're looking for that's changed.*

They sob, cupping his face in their hands. *Bro, you have to conquer the wave of your own resistance. You have to shred your earthly fears.*

Right, says the Midwestern Man. *So there's all that.* He pulls out his bandanna to wipe his neck & his forehead & his shins. *Also, I'm sweating balls.*

At the bus station, the Midwestern Man sees the Southern Woman. *You, too?* he asks. The Southern Woman laughs until she's wiping tears from her eyes. *Oh, honey,* she says. *Please.*

The country passes him by through the windows of a bus. A young girl clutches his hand, leans across him for a better view. *What do you think?* she asks.

The Midwestern Man studies his hands. The young girl traces his callouses as she scans the sky.
Good, strong hands. But what would they be when his wife expected words? *Useless.* Just that.

It has occurred to him that his wife is not the type to wallow.
That she may have missed him, mourned him, then forgotten.

She may have found a new husband, one who would never, ever leave.
They might have children now, in a cookie-cutter house. A snow blower & a concrete drive.

He sighs deeply & considers the endless wave of prairie, the cracking blue-gray sky.
Looks fine, he says. He nods & pats the small girl's head. *Looks just fine.*

At long last the Midwestern Man steps off the bus & breathes the Midwestern air.
Hot dog, he says. *I'm home.*

In town, some folks are happy to see him; others pretend. None of them look the least surprised.
They all look pretty much the same, the Midwestern Man thinks. Plus or minus a few years.

The Midwestern Man had dreamt of his secluded home: his winding dirt path, his barrier of pine.
But from 'round the bluff, he sees the trees are thin & spare, the land behind them far too open.

There's no longer a home there.
Nothing—just some tall grass & a few mounds of dirt.

When he gets closer, he sees the mounds of dirt aren't mounds of dirt at all.
They're pyramids of lumber, piles of shingles & nails. A cinderblock tower stacked clean & tall.

A small wooden box sits in the woodstove's place. The Midwestern Man kneels in front of it.
Inside, there's an afghan blanket, a hammer & a note.

Nice horse, the note says. The hammer is a little rusted.
The blanket is the one they shared.

The Midwestern Man lies back on his lawn. His once beautiful lawn, now wild and overgrown.
He removes his cap. *Hot for summer here*, he thinks. The breeze feels nice.

A doe & her fawn walk into the clearing to graze.
Someone came & thinned his forest. Still the deer surprise him when they step out of the trees.

Family, he thinks. He bows his head. The Midwestern Man was prepared for this, he thought.
But he had no way of knowing how devastated he would be.

Still, there's this box. He smiles & examines the build.
Not so badly crafted, really. Not so amateur at all. It's a gift, a beautiful gift.

Still, he has his land to tend & rebuild.
There, a garden. There, a spot to sit & whittle. There, a pit to sit around a fire.

And if he listens closely, he realizes, he can hear the water. Had he never noticed it before?
He can hear the calm lake waves sliding over the shore.

His old hunting buddies will soon come running. They'll all ride quads & float down the river.
He'll have his town & his woods & his crik & his—

He waits for it, but the ache never comes.
All right then, says the Midwestern Man.

In the dirt beneath the box he sketches a blueprint. He sweeps it clean & tries again—larger.
Larger for the family room, larger for the bedroom, larger for the kitchen.

He pulls up grass to make more dirt. His sketch grows larger & larger.
A guest room & a dining room & a basement bar. In his mind, he fills the rooms.

The Midwestern Man stands and surveys the land, the piles of his old life. The job ahead of him.
It's his job. There's help if he needs it, but it's his job & his alone.

Builds character, thinks the Midwestern Man.
And he believes it, he damn sure does.

The Professorial Anteater Rises Above & Beyond His Working-Class Background

"Consider the anteater," the Professorial Anteater says, in front of a class of hundreds for the first time. His voice, too nasally, is lost inside the hallowed walls of the hallowed hall. The pointer slips from his long fore claws & a single drop of sweat stains the collar of his newly fitted suit.

The Modern City Anteater is Nocturnal

He imports his ants—fresh, not frozen. He eats them with a glass of wine, a book of poetry, Tchaikovsky on the record player he wishes was antique, inheritance from a grandfather who might have taught him to lower the needle with grace. The Modern City Anteater paints best in silence, lives best in the quiet hours before dawn, before he sleeps through the bright day & wakes to meals delivered to his doorstep without fail, express from Colombia or Brazil. For nights on end, the Modern City Anteater loses himself in his work, productive in the absence of human noise—so productive, in fact, he occasionally wakes in early evening to an empty porch, realizing with dread he's mismanaged his deliveries, that, in his flurry of creative output, he's forgotten to renew his order of imported ants. The Modern City Anteater considers drunkenness unfashionable, but on the nights he must lumber outside to his apartment courtyard's one small patch of grass & forage for sour insects in the city-tainted soil, the Modern City Anteater drinks to forget.

The Suburban Anteater Dad is, at Worst, a Serviceable Youth Basketball Coach & A Middling Sculptor of Impressionable Young Minds

He doesn't yell, at least—not when the young men launch reckless 3-pointers mere seconds into possessions, not when they mock his inability to properly demonstrate a bounce pass. When his guidance is met with insult, he takes the offending young player aside & addresses him with patience & respect. *Do not as I do, nor as I say. But ask yourself: How would I feel if my team only remembered me for this one single act?* The Suburban Anteater Dad places both claws on the young player's shoulders and stares into his eyes. *Ask yourself: How would I feel if my team only remembered me for this one single act?* says the Suburban Anteater Dad. *My family, my species, my place in the world?*

The Young Anteater is Uncomfortable in His Body

He dulls his claws & folds them to his wrists, wishes they'd retract. He trims & clips his brush feather tail. He Googles *edentate*, opens & closes the tip of his snout, dreaming of what it means to chew. The Young Anteater is embarrassed to run outside. He spends evening after evening lumbering on the treadmill's slowest speed, knuckles pocking rubber. The Young Anteater is portly. The Young Anteater wears glasses that never stay up. It is no laughing matter—many young anteaters never learn to laugh.

The Angry Giant Anteater Takes the Subway

His every step is a dare, a reminder of his size, how much of this small space could be his if he wanted. When young men in baseball caps stare too long, so lithe & smooth & tiny, he hooks them by their ear buds & yanks the cord from their phones. *What the fuck do I look like to you?* he asks. *An anteater*, they say. The Angry Giant Anteater lifts himself off the gum-stuck floor & flexes. *You're goddamn right.*

The Bachelor Anteater is Capable of Love, Though He Rarely Pursues It

His friends & coworkers mate for life, but the Bachelor Anteater can't break from his hardwired custom—or he can't find the one to break it with. His affairs are brief, though not meaningless. Afterward, as she drifts to sleep in his apartment, he lies awake imagining the weight of a newborn on his back. Juvenile claw marks on the furniture, coarse hair sheared short or dyed in rebellion. He dreams of a different routine—the bed shifting with the familiar mass of another slowly climbing up to meet him. It's wrong to feel this way, the Bachelor Anteater knows, but worse to feel it alone. He plans to tell her when she wakes, to risk himself, finally sharing the twin burdens of doubt & hope that haunt him, but when he opens his eyes to sunlight, she is gone, she has left nothing but her imprint on the mattress.

Good Christians Want to Save the Scaly Anteater, the Anteater's Cousin, Who is Hardly an Anteater at All

God's finest handiwork, they call him—the lurching, cat-sized pine cone. The tiny, toothless dog dragon. The shingled dinosaur that stumbles, ungodly, on its two hind legs.

The Scaly Anteater wanders foreign cities in search of kinship. *We can help you find others*, whisper cruel, sinful men from the shadows of their stores. *We can tell you where.*

When he's easily pried from his scaly ball—an impenetrable defense against lions & tigers, predators without tools—and sees the pot of water to boil his scales, the knives to pierce him, the vials to hold his blood; & when he imagines how the cruel, sinful men will sell his body, the ways he will be crushed & inhaled as aphrodisiac & cure, the Scaly Anteater, for the first time, tries to pray.

The Impoverished Anteater Isn't Proud of his Past

Though he misses the power of standing so tall, propped against *his* brick wall in *his* alley, customers completely reliant. He misses controlling their bodies. He misses knowing his dope was surfing through their bloodstreams. He misses staring the men away from his tail, the way they looked at him when they realized he, only he, could make them whole.

The Country Anteater Finds Peace

It's not true the air is clean—he can still smell fire across the savannah—but he finds comfort in the fresh, pure dirt that flavors his meals: mounds of wild termites he crushes & swallows, ant hills he rips open with his claws. He is happy & he is alone, one anteater body in a massive world, & despite the lurking predators, he's not afraid. When the night is soft & the space is wide, he toes his own invented line & begins to amble, at first with blissful leisure, then picking up speed, faster, faster yet, as fast as he's ever moved, his claws churning dirt, eucalyptus and baobab blurring in his periphery, faster, he is sure, than any man or beast has ever moved, a speed he is sure he wasn't meant to reach & he is certain, in that moment, as he breaks the laws that once ruled his body, that he runs with flawless form.

The South-Bound Train

Two trains approach each other in the night. One train is heading north & the other is heading south. Both have traveled a long, long ways & both are traveling very, very fast.

I mean, they are really chugging along.

They come across a great big hill & start to climb it. They chug & they creak & they groan. Their cargo shifts & rattles. Then at the top the two trains come to a grinding halt, right next to each other.

Whoa, says the North-Bound Train. You don't look so hot.

Oof, says the South-Bound Train. I feel a little queasy.

You should stop and rest a while, says the North-Bound Train.

O yes, says the South-Bound Train. But I can't very well stop. I have a schedule to keep.

The North-Bound Train laughs. You must be new to this, he says.

Well, yes, says the South-Bound Train. Actually, I am.

Please, says the North-Bound Train. Stop & rest & talk to me a while. I'd hate to think of you out there all alone, feeling so ill.

The South-Bound Train smiles a little.

Well, she says. I guess I do have just a few minutes
to spare.

So, he says, where you headed?

South, she says.

Well whaddaya know, says the North-Bound Train.
I just came from there.

I've got lumber, he says. And you?

O, I don't know, she says. Just some coal, I guess.

Well, says the South-Bound Train. I guess I should be
going.

Are you feeling better? asks the North-Bound Train.

Yes, she says. It's just—oh, never mind.

What? he says. You can talk to me.

It's just all this north & south & north & south, she
says.

O yes, he chuckles. It's not for everyone.

I knew this job would be hard, she says. But I just
didn't think I'd feel so...trapped.

The North-Bound Train thinks for a moment.

What do you call a train that eats too much toffee?
he says.

I don't know, she says.

A chew chew train, he says.

And the South-Bound Train laughs so hard & long
the rest of her trip goes by like *that*.

A few weeks pass & the South-Bound Train can't stop

thinking about the North-Bound Train. Whenever she across upon a hill, she puts everything she has into it, racing all the way up as fast as she can.

Of course she wants to stop & talk to the North-Bound Train the next time she sees him. She just wants to do it on her own terms.

But when the two trains finally meet again, at the same spot at the top of the same hill, she's once again winded.

Well, hello there stranger, says the North-Bound Train.

Just give me a second, says the South-Bound Train.

So, says the North-Bound Train. What do you want to talk about? If you are feeling well enough to talk.

O, I feel fine, says the South-Bound Train.

That's good, he says.

Yes, I just like to take a break, she says. Here. Sometimes.

It *is* nice, he says. To take breaks.

And they rest together in silence for a while.

I was in your neck of the woods the other day, says the South-Bound Train.

O yes, says the North-Bound Train.

It's beautiful, she says.

O yes, he says.

Have you traveled all around? she asks. Out west, maybe? I'd really love to go. I even dream about it sometimes.

And it's true—in her dreams it's *zip, zoom* & she's flying free down the coastline, watching surfers zigzag the waves.

O yes, he says. I've been all over.

Is it wonderful? she asks. The West?

O, he says. O yes.

The two sit in silence for a while. They really have nothing to talk about.

Say, says the North-Bound Train. Did you ever hear the joke—

But just then, a noise interrupts him. It's a voice—a person.

Would you two quit wailing at each other already?

It's a woman—she's trapped between them, with no clear way around.

Excuse me? says the North-Bound Train.

I said move it, chump, says the woman.

Well, says the North-Bound Train. That's very rude.

That's very rude, the woman says.

I'm just saying, he says.

I'm just saying, she says.

Stop that, he says.

And the woman flips him the bird.

Listen, says the South-Bound Train. We should go. I mean, we *are* kind of in her way.

I've got a plane to catch, says the woman. You hear that? *A plane.*

Not a chance, says the North-Bound Train. Not until she asks nicely.

Oof, says the South-Bound Train. Really?

You sonofabitch, says the woman. How 'bout I kick your ass instead?

O! says the North-Bound Train. I'd like to see you try!

The woman winds up & kicks him with all her might. Her foot *dings* the steel boxcar & she hops all around, howling in pain.

There, says the North-Bound Train. *Now* we can leave.

Ugh, says the South-Bound Train.

A few more weeks pass & the South-Bound Train really starts to get the hang of things. She becomes much faster & stronger & she rarely gets tired. Pretty soon, she's clearing mountains with ease.

The next time she sees the North-Bound Train, she's already coasting downhill while he's still climbing up. She's going so fast, she hardly recognizes him.

Whooooaaaaa, he says. Heyyyyyyyy. He grinds on his brakes & wails hello.

But *whoosh*. She just rumbles right on past.

Sometimes when the South-Bound Train hauls her cargo South, she feels terribly sad. It's just the same boring route—the same mountains & rivers & trees she knows by heart.

On every trip, at the bottom of the big hill where

she first met the North-Bound Train, the South-Bound Train passes a valley she can almost see. She can tell by the smell it's filled with blooming flowers & every time she passes by, she imagines what color, what kind, what it might be like to ride through that beautiful, fragrant field. But then the rail jerks her away & it's back to the same dirt mounds, the same factories & bridges & walls.

When the night shift workers unload her cargo, she wonders: What's it all for, anyway?

And when she heads back up the other way, empty, she feels even worse.

What even *am* I right now? she asks herself.

Just a lonesome train, she answers. Just a lonely, lonesome train.

Waaaawwwwwwwhhh, she wails, loud & soulful into the unreceptive mountains. Waaaaaaaaawwwhhh, comes her own voice back at her.

And it's just like that, the whole way up.

One day, the South-Bound Train comes to where she first met the North-Bound Train. Except this time she sees the woman instead.

Heyyyyyyyy, says the South-Bound Train.

Oh, it's you, says the woman. Have you come to wail back & forth with your boyfriend some more?

O, him? says the South-Bound Train. No, I don't talk to *him* anymore.

Nice, says the woman.

How was your trip? asks the South-Bound Train. On

the airplane, I mean.

The woman hangs her head & sighs. I didn't go, she says. As it turns out, I'm afraid of flying.

O, I see, says the South-Bound Train. Me, too, she adds.

I'm such a coward, says the woman. I've wanted to leave this crummy town my entire life! Move somewhere by the ocean, maybe tend bar at one of those seaside resorts. But I've never even left the state. Every time I try, I just end up wimping out & turning around.

O my, says the South-Bound Train. That's terrible.

I know, says the woman. I'm sorry I got so mad at your boyfriend. It's just that sometimes—

Sometimes what? says the South-Bound Train. You can talk to me.

Sometimes I just feel so...trapped, says the woman.

Suddenly the South-Bound Train has an idea.

I'm heading West, she says. And her saying it makes it true. You should come with me, she says.

O, West, says the woman. Is nice out there? Is it really worth the trip?

The South-Bound Train has heard stories. In the West, she'll never freeze or rust. In the West, she'll be cool & free. In the West, she'll haul fresh timber or maybe even nothing at all. Maybe she'll just ride as she pleases, this way or that.

But the woman makes her doubt herself. Maybe she hadn't even heard those stories. Maybe they were just from her dreams.

O, I don't know, she says. I've only ever gone the one

way or the other. Maybe we should just stay here instead.

The woman thinks for a moment. Then she pulls a bandanna from her pocket & uses it to corral her hair.

Yeehaw! she says as she hops on. The South-Bound Train wails a happy wail.

The South-Bound Train & the woman travel South for a while.

This isn't working, yells the woman.

So the South-Bound Train begins to pick up speed. She puts everything she has into it, chugging faster & faster & up a great big hill. Then she realizes it's *her* hill. And at the bottom is *her* valley, the one she could only ever almost see.

Hold on, she wails & she veers toward the valley with all her might.

She hops the rails & she & the woman take flight.

The
Guava
Man

A young couple didn't fight often, but whenever small disagreements occurred it was their practice for the offending party to offer a gift of guava as a sign of repentance.

Neither the young husband nor the young wife could remember precisely when this tradition had been conceived. In fact, neither of them could remember ever acknowledging the tradition to the other. It was, the young husband and wife decided, just one of those things.

Sorry, said the guava in the young husband's briefcase. Sorry, said the guava in the bread box. Good morning, said the guava next to the coffeepot on the counter. Also, Sorry.

If the young husband was hesitant to admit an offense—a fault, the young wife's married friends assured her, that was not uncommon among husbands of any age—the young wife's anger would subside, replaced instead by a gnawing worry that this time, for the first time, her guava wouldn't come.

The young wife would search all the places she was accustomed to receiving apologies, fretful that her own inability to find the guava would be an offense all its own—that she, too, would need to purchase a guava to apologize for the cool and aloof persona she had constructed in response to her husband's offense. That now it was her fault, that her sweet young husband had already issued a tender apology she was simply too daft to see. On such occasions, the young husband would find his wife hovering nervously in the kitchen or the hall and embrace her from behind, placing the guava directly in her hand—a gesture both parties found intimate and quaint.

These apologies never went to waste, for the couple would eat each guava together—the offended cutting the fruit and feeding it to the offender—to show that all had been forgiven. The young wife made guava juice, guava jelly, guava cream cheese and guava pastries. She dried the guava and used it for glazes, for salads, for ice creams.

The young couple was simply mad about guavas.

They even had a guava man, a mustachioed fruit vendor with a fruit cart downtown near the lake, just a short walk from the young couple's home.

One guava, please, the offending party would say.

Oh, you two, the Guava Man would tsk.

The young husband was a businessman, and an especially successful one considering his age. Lauded by peers and superiors alike as an emerging leader in his field, he was granted numerous opportunities to travel widely, within the country and abroad, as a representative of his company. Foreign partners were consistently impressed by the young businessman's poise.

The young wife worked locally, and while she was proud of her husband's accomplishments, she was too often frustrated by his irregular communication while away on business. She was not accustomed to being alone, and even less accustomed to being ignored. Kind as the young wife was, there were limits to her patience.

Once, when the young husband failed to keep in contact during a taxing weeklong trip across the world, his oversight prompted the young couple's most serious fight.

It's like you abandon me, the young wife said. You leave and become another person and you don't need me at all.

It's my job, the young husband stammered. I need my briefcase. I need my phone.

You need your clothes washed. You need your lawn watered, the young wife said. What am I supposed to do, work and clean and sit around and wait for you?

Well, said the young husband. And then he didn't quite know what to say. He did miss his wife when he was away. He missed her terribly. It was a relief to come home to her—to trimmed hedges, yes, the wind-dried linen, yes, though all he really expected was his beautiful wife in the doorway to take in his arms. She, to him, was home.

Instead of saying all that, the young husband instead reached into his luggage and presented his wife with an apology he'd hoped he wouldn't need.

What is this? the young wife asked.

A dragon fruit.

A dragon fruit?

The young husband picked a knife from a counter and sliced through the near-fluorescent skin to reveal a pale and seedy flesh.

A dragon fruit, he said.

When the young couple enjoyed extended periods of marital bliss, as young couples are wont to do, the Guava Man did not forget about them.

He did not wish misfortune on anyone—certainly not on happy young couples—but there was no denying that his business suffered without their quarrels. After all, guavas are not often in high demand, except by the people who love them.

Whenever the Guava Man saw the young husband or young wife walking toward his stand after an extended absence, he sprung from his chair and repositioned the guavas in his stand. He flicked the streamers dangling from the canopy, making them spin and glimmer in the sun. His mustache danced and waved hello.

Where have you been? the Guava Man would ask.

Happy, the young husband or wife would say.

Oh, you two, the Guava Man would tsk.

It was a long time after the dragon fruit before the young couple fought again.

Though the young couple had not been married long, they did not consider their happiness a symptom of a honeymoon period or any such span of blind newlywed bliss—a delusion that amused their married friends, who assured the young couple their happy defiance was a clear sign they were indeed in such a phase. But for the young wife it was more complicated. After the dragon fruit, she felt the presence of something new in their relationship, some intrusion that had rendered foreign their system of offense and absolution.

The young wife worried about the meaning of the dragon fruit. If she should offend her husband now, what would he expect of her? Would he take her guava as insincere?

The guava system had been a good one for the young couple. With she being a quiet woman and he a quiet man, the two of them trusted their ability to communicate in quiet ways, affirming their rightness for each other in touches and gestures. But now the young wife feared that what her husband was expressing was not simply an apology but something different altogether. She feared that the young husband had seen enough of the world to be bored with the small, quiet life he kept at home, to be bored with her. She worried he thought of their life as a mute life, a life of repeating offenses.

Is everything OK? the young wife asked, interrupting their evening reading time.

What? The young husband peered over the top of his newspaper.

I said, is everything all right?

Yes, of course.

And there's nothing wrong?

No, no, nothing wrong, the young husband said, smiling. Everything all right and nothing wrong.

Still, the young wife worried. She was certain there were other questions she should have been asking—questions she should have already asked.

Are you angry?

Of course not. Why would I be?

Was dinner all right?

Yes, of course, said the young husband.

Are you sure?

Yes, said the young husband, looking back to his newspaper and shifting in his chair. I already said it was.

Is reclining like that the best thing for your back, do you think?

Would you stop picking at me? the young husband snipped.

He kicked his recliner down, wincing slightly, and tossed his newspaper to the floor. He walked down the hallway and, as young husbands are wont to do, slammed his office door.

The Guava Man jumped to attention when the young wife approached his stand. He shuffled through the guavas on display, placing the best ones at the top of the pile. He picked three guavas from the cart and started juggling the fruit.

Where have you been? the Guava Man said, laughing. I have been all alone with my guavas.

Hello, said the young wife, only briefly meeting the Guava Man's eyes. She hunched her shoulders and walked quickly past the stand.

On her way back, she kept her eyes straight ahead, ignoring the Guava Man's pyramid of guavas. She crossed one arm over her stomach to hide the bulge in her jacket as she passed.

What's this? the young husband asked.

Kiwi, the young wife said.

Kiwi?

The young husband stood with the fruit in his hand for a long time—long enough for the young wife to fear that her daring move had failed, that this single fruit was deviant enough to break the system they'd created together. Before her husband could speak, the young wife picked a knife from the kitchen drawer and placed it gently in his hand. Apologetically, she thought. Coyly, she hoped.

After what seemed like many hours, the young husband smiled and kissed his wife. He reached back into the drawer for a spoon, and the two shared the kiwi until only the skin remained.

It was a good kiwi, the young wife thought, but it was certainly no guava.

Well, the young husband thought. Kiwi.

Downtown, the other fruit cart vendors teased the Guava Man. They resented him for the way he drew potential customers to his stand with juggling tricks and acrobatic displays. While the Guava Man's business was struggling, his theatrics kept him in competition with peddlers of more popular fruits.

The vendors on fruit row were the latest in a long line of fruit men, many carrying on a tradition that went back three generations or more. Though the Guava Man had claimed his territory many years ago, and though he had proven himself to be nothing if not neighborly to his companions on fruit row, the other men still thought him an intruder and a nuisance—more a cheap, flashy showman than a true fruit man. Though they hid their animosity in humor, they rarely passed on a chance to rub salt in his fruity wounds.

All your business is gone, they said. They laughed and slapped each others' backs. Soon you will be more broke than the rest of us!

Everything is all right, the Guava Man said, smiling and patting his fruit. He plucked the stem from a baseball-sized guava and tossed it from hand to hand.

Remember, the vendors said, wagging their fingers, you are an old man. It will not be so easy finding a new line of work for a man as old as you.

No, no, nothing is wrong, the Guava Man said. Everything all right and nothing wrong.

The young couple learned that bliss was not guaranteed with marriage—that it was possible for chaos to infiltrate their lives without warning, quietly and completely.

Kiwis gave way to papayas, papayas gave way to sugar apples, sugar apples gave way to cherimoyas. Plums turned to breadfruit turned to mangoes turned to salmonberry. Star fruit to cactus fruit to jackfruit and jujubes.

The young wife joined an Exotic Fruit of the Month club, and boxes of peculiar produce soon lined the living-room walls. The young husband experimented with botany, and his office bookshelves were soon overgrown with vines.

The young couple's relationship had been founded on their ability to understand each other's desires and, more important, their confidence that each was well-suited to satisfy the wants of the other. But now their marriage was laced with paranoia, second-guessing at every turn. Both parties were certain they were guilty of a thousand small offenses, of gifting fruits spoiled by malice or disgust. Both parties were certain their apologies had been denied.

When they spoke, they spoke only in fruits.

Banana strawberry, the young husband pleaded.

Blueberry peach, the young wife insisted, though her husband's words did not leave her unmoved.

Tensions mounted as the fruit stacked higher. Plums dropped at random, seemingly from the sky. A web of bluish mold crept from the refrigerator and carpeted the walls.

The young husband emptied the young wife's perfume and instead filled the bottle with a chokeberry extract that colored her red. The next morning, he opened his closet door and was buried by a mound of persimmons.

Persimmons, the young husband gasped. By God!

The young husband placed chunks of durian in all the young wife's shoes. The next morning, he rolled off the bed and nearly drowned in a vat of elderberry preserves.

At first, the young husband obliged these exchanges with only a small degree of annoyance, but grew increasingly angry with each of the young wife's responses. When he stopped offering fruit altogether and the young wife did not follow suit, each bushel of pears or pillowcase of kumquats spurred a whole new level of rage.

The young husband constructed a barricade of plums around his chair, but the young wife had already sprinkled blackberries in the crevices of the seat. He crafted a barrier of pineapples in the bed between them, but still he woke with pawpaws on his navel. Still, when he thought he was alone in his cave of apricots, he found handfuls of boysenberries in the pockets of his favorite slacks.

Boysenberries, the young husband sobbed, purple dribbling down his hand.

Finally the young husband burst through his cocoon of plantains and gathered all the fruit that had been gifted to him. He filled bushels with kumquats and persimmons from the bedroom, emptied the pockets of his sport coats to find berries of all origins. He cleared the linen closet of grapes, bagged the citrus from the shower, cradled an armful of cantaloupes from beneath the bathroom sink.

The young husband arranged a ring of fruit around him in the kitchen, then sat down in the middle with a knife in his hand. He picked a lime from a bucket, cut in, and began to eat.

What are you doing? the young wife asked. The young husband didn't answer, for his mouth was full of lime.

When the young husband finished the limes, he started on the bushel of pears, eating even the cores. After the pears, the kumquats. After the kumquats, the persimmons, then red grapes by the cluster.

The young wife stood by and watched, waiting for either of them to ask the question that hung around the house more stubbornly than the fruit flies.

You'll make yourself sick, is all she finally said.

The young husband hawked the stem of a grape in response.

Finally, the young husband sliced straight through an orange and into his palm, spattering red the rinds and seeds and skin around him. He dropped the knife and howled a terrible howl.

Your hand! the young wife gasped, rushing to his side.

The young husband's eyes filled with tears. He clutched his bloody hand with his good one and stomped the floor in pain and frustration.

Are you OK? the young wife asked. She knelt beside him and stroked his back. In her other hand she held a single, perfect avocado.

The young husband, on the verge of an outburst for weeks, finally lost his temper. He tore at the already-splintered crates and bushels, dented the appliances with wild and furious kicks. He spat irreparable offenses in the face of his once-lovely wife, now crippled with tears.

The young husband stood up in the gaudy carnage, walked to the bedroom, and packed a backpack full of clothes. He stomped back through the kitchen and paused, still heaving angry breaths, his wife still flattened by tears, before slinging his bag over his shoulder and walking out the door.

• • •

Without the patronage of the young couple, the Guava Man's business slowed to a near halt. The other vendors' once-boisterous jokes turned to furtive whispers. They seized the opportunity to speak ill of the Guava Man, to steer his prospective customers away.

Look at him standing there, all alone, they said, snapping men and women out of their juggle-induced glaze. If he has not one regular customer, how can he be trusted? Surely, some contamination has been discovered. Surely, his guavas are defective.

The Guava Man smiled and waved and patted his guavas, as he was wont to do. Occasionally he leaned back and loosed a belly laugh, a welcoming gesture for all to come and join him, to enjoy life as it was meant to be enjoyed: with guavas, of course.

But his regular customers hesitated, then walked quickly past.

His guavas, the other vendors whispered, they are simply no good.

The Guava Man watched the people pass with great confusion. He picked a guava from the pile and held it in his palm. Guava? he asked. He cleared his throat; his voice held nothing of its normal panache. Guava, please?

You will find better guavas elsewhere, the other vendors entreated. Anywhere elsewhere. Perhaps even here. With this, they would wave a hand over their own carts, now stocked to the brim with guavas—a territory the fruit men had respected before.

Tell me, they said. Have you ever seen guavas like these?

The Guava Man, increasingly feverish in his

attempts to attract new customers, began juggling the fruit. He was oblivious to the treachery of his peers; his vision was obscured by the rise and fall of guavas.

After weeks without a sale, the poverty-stricken Guava Man was forced to auction his cart to the conglomerate of fruit men, who used his vacated lot to doubly stock their wares. Refusing their offer to dispose of his leftover guavas, the Guava Man emptied his stock—now soft with age—into a burlap sack he hoisted over his shoulder.

The Guava Man cut such a pathetic figure with his bag of fruit and wilted mustache that the other fruit men couldn't pass on a chance to torment him more.

Come out and drink with us one last time, they pleaded, though it was the first time they had extended such an invitation.

No, no, the Guava Man said. I couldn't do that.

You are worried about money? the fruit men asked. Well, you should be! But not tonight. Tonight, the Guava Man drinks on us.

No, no, it's not about that, the Guava Man said. It's not about that at all.

The young once-wife was wrecked by her husband's departure.

She passed her days in mourning, leaving the house only at midday to run short, violent loops around her neighborhood in her city by the lake. At night she lay in bed, retracing the events that led to the young once-couple's separation. She wracked her brain for what she could have done differently, tried desperately to pinpoint the fatal error that led to their demise. But, try as she might, the young once-wife never found answers. Her memory of the relationship's decline was warped and fuzzy, somehow incomplete.

Under the pressure of heat and age, the fruit still in boxes seeped out and colored the floors. Pulpy bits spread and festered. Unkempt, the house began to decompose.

For so long the young once-wife had kept a home fit for a family. But now the house was marred with fruit-stink failure. Now the house was much too large.

For two years they lived apart, these past lovers of fruit and of each other. The young once-wife settled into a daily routine as she grew more comfortable living alone. Healing happened over time, slow and unspectacular. The young once-wife scrubbed the house until there was no trace of the fruit that had once meant love and forgiveness, then, later, confusion and regret.

The young once-wife ran longer and harder, always at the hottest part of the day, not failing to notice how it benefited her appetite. When her husband first left, she hadn't been able to choke down even the smallest meal. Running made her ravenous. After a workout was the only time she ate freely.

The young once-wife's appetite balanced as time passed. By the third year, she arrived home from her runs completely spent and ate without bingeing. She began planning all of her meals, assembling them item by item during her weekly trips to the grocery store.

Bravely, she thought, and magnanimously, she hoped, she ventured to the fruit aisle.

She offered and accepted an apology of her own.

During the period of the young once-couple's separation, the Guava Man lived as a nomad whose range was the stuff of lore. One morning he'd be sighted at the northeast corner of the metropolis, then spotted not an hour later at the opposite end. There were reported Guava Man sightings on rooftops and in backyards, in construction zones and sewers. The Guava Man was only seen on foot, unprotected from the elements, trekking city sidewalks with his burlap sack. Some insisted he was a cursed man, walking the earth for penance, while others were certain he was on a pilgrimage. A select few swore he was a disgraced former political figure in disguise. One woman insisted the Guava Man had saved her child from choking without even breaking stride. Another man was convinced the Guava Man had wandered into an auditorium and delivered a conference keynote that made grown men fall to their knees and weep.

Some thought the Guava Man was lost, but others insisted there was a pattern to his wandering, that he walked the big city street by street in monthlong loops. Since the Guava Man was always moving, seeing him more than once was a rarity. Those who witnessed multiple viewings wanted to claim the Guava Man as a native of the city, while others insisted he had come from afar—an outcast, a nomad, a man who couldn't call any place home.

There was rampant speculation on the contents of the Guava Man's sack, the most observant citizens noting the pinkish trail of liquid that followed in his wake. Some fearless children even went so far as to ask him directly what was in the bag, but the Guava Man only smiled at them weakly and continued to walk. He stared at each stranger with a look of desperation and restraint, as if he was as likely to beg them for money as to pitch them a sale.

Packs of drunken fruit men searched high and low for The Guava Man, tracking him by his sticky trail. The city police had come for their licenses, and the vendors hadn't made a sale in months. At night, the bitter horde descended upon the Guava Man in the alleys where he slept and blitzed him with rotting fruit.

Give up the guavas, the men yelled in a blackout rage, but the Guava Man cradled his burlap sack tight to his chest. He curled up and weathered each assault until eventually the men, fruitless and bored, would stumble away.

Often the youngish woman ate dinner alone, but occasionally she had her evening meals in the company of visitors. Whichever evenings the youngish woman's married friends visited, the three dined without hesitation or reserve. The youngish woman discovered new recipes and cooked elaborate dishes. She ate until she was satisfied.

But on some nights, when she was alone, the youngish woman paused in her seat before serving herself, as if she was praying or waiting for the company of another. On those nights, she picked at her plate slowly, tossing far more than she ate.

One day the Guava Man woke not to a pack of fruit men around him, but a youngish man in a sport coat and a creased pair of jeans. The youngish man wore his hair cut short, and a smattering of cuts flecked his stubbled face, as if that morning's shave had been a heroic undertaking. It was a face that looked much older than a youngish man's should, but the Guava Man recognized him at once.

Where have you been? the Guava Man asked. He jumped to his feet, his face once again familiarizing itself with the arc of a smile. He patted the youngish man's shoulders and arms and hopped excitedly from side to side.

I've been looking for you, the youngish man said, for a long time.

For me! the Guava Man said.

The youngish man smiled a worldly smile.

First they said you were far, he said. Then they said you were near.

You've come for my guavas, the Guava Man beamed.

Can you help me? the youngish man asked.

What do I look like? the Guava Man asked.

He reached into the sack on his shoulder and extracted from it a perfectly taut, green guava—fresh as the day it was picked.

Though the woman was surprised by the appearance of the man at her porch, she invited him inside. After all, she was still a kind woman—perhaps even kinder than before—and while the days of her mourning had long passed, certainly she had loved him once, and certainly she had missed him even after that love had wilted. Certainly she still saw him in the body of this new man, more haggard and restrained.

The man and the woman sat down together and talked themselves into tears, into laugher, into a remembrance that wasn't nostalgia or regret, but simply a mutual recognition that they had grown and killed a life together.

Then, when the time seemed right, the man reached into his pocket. Shyly, carefully, he set the guava on the table.

Well, the woman said. Guava.

The man and the woman sat at the table for a long time with the guava between them.

Elsewhere in the city, the Guava Man walked on—his sack one guava lighter, but still heavy enough to weigh him down.

Love Stories

1

Two tarps meet on a road.

The road is long & busy & wide, but they are the only two tarps on the road.

One tarp is faster than the other.

Hello, the slow tarp waves.

Hello, the fast tarp whips its reply. It weaves ahead of the slow tarp & into the hills.

The slow tarp is charmed. It's been a long time since it has seen another tarp, especially one so fast & so clean. It thinks about the fast tarp all the way through the mountains & across the plains. When the slow tarp reaches the ocean, it unbuckles at the shore. It takes a deep breath.

The fast tarp continues to wave long after it passes. It whips & turns & writhes itself into ripples & bunches, desperate to see if the slow tarp had been watching, if the slow tarp had seen.

The fast tarp waves & waves & flies faster, up a mountain, down a mountain, up again, alone.

The fast tarp waves & waves until it is gutted by the wind.

2

Two anteaters meet at a feast.

They amuse each other.

One anteater tells the other anteater a joke, a little known fact about aphrodisiacs.

No way, says one anteater.

Yes way, says the other.

They eat ants together. Ants on ants on ants. One is a slow ant eater & the other is fast.

Hey, slow down, says the slow ant eater. The fast ant eater laughs.

The anteaters feast until all the ants are gone. When the land dries up, some humans come & burn the savannah.

The fast anteater escapes. It runs to the top of a hill and looks down to where the slow anteater is ambling away from the fire.

Faster, the fast anteater calls.

The slow anteater runs as fast as it can.

The slow anteater runs very slowly.

Run faster, the fast anteater calls.

The slow anteater thinks, *I am*, & is eaten by the fire.

3

Paul is a runner who runs a lot of miles.

He runs a lot of races against runners who also run a lot of miles—some even more than him.

Paul memorizes the names of all the other runners in his races. He starts at the back of the pack & passes every runner until he is in first place. The other runners know that he is saying their names because they hear him whispering as he passes.

Once, after Paul wins a long, hard race, he is approached for an interview.

How do you do it? the newspaperman asks. *How do you run so fast?*

Paul says: *Michael, Michael, Michael, Michael, Michael, Michael, Michael, Michael.*

4

Two hills are born of the same valley.

They grow up side by side. One hill comes in at a lean & tickles the other. The valley between the two hills is very thin. People walk around them & never between.

Together, the two hills watch seventeen thousand, three-hundred & fifty-one sunsets.

Then one day the hills begin growing wide instead of tall. They push against each other from a space that is buried, a deep space where they had once been twined.

The dip between them spreads itself smooth.

Maybe this is for the best, says one hill.

Maybe, says the other.

A tremor pushes them meters apart, then miles.

One hill grows much larger than the other. It stretches wide & tall & towers over a new valley, a new city, people who call it mountain.

The small hill stays where it has always stayed.

One day, the small hill sends a messenger to deliver a message to the big hill, now many sunsets away.

The messenger is loyal, but soon finds himself lost. He wanders for days until a blizzard hits the messenger & buries him with the message on his breath.

The small hill waits where it has always waited.

It thinks, *How far we must have drifted.*

The mountain looks over its new valley, its new city,

the people climbing up its side.
      It thinks, *How far I have come.*

5

A skeleton sleeps for a long time.
    He wakes & picks a hair from his eye.
    This isn't mine, he says.

6

A lover writes a letter to his lover, promising to change.

The letter also writes a letter. It writes a letter to the letter it will become when the lover's lover reads her lover's letter. When the lover's lover understands who her lover has become.

The lover's love isn't the same love, then, but a different one, changed by her lover's letter, changed by the lover's letter's letter into someone new.

The new lover writes back.

The new lover's letter also writes a letter to the lover's letter's letter, to the letter it once was.

The new lover's letter says, *I'm sorry.*

The new lover's letter's letter says, *I am still confused.*

7

A woman says to a man, *I love you.*
The man can only squeeze her hand.

ACKNOWLEDGEMENTS

Thank you to Joseph Demes, Joshua Bohnsack and everyone at Long Day Press for putting these weird little stories out into the world.

Thank you to the editors at publications where versions of these stories have been previously published: Tara Laskowski at *Smokelong Quarterly* ("This is What I know About Being Gigantic"); Madeleine Maillet and Bükem Reitmayer at *Cosmonauts Avenue* ("The Grandmothers"); Tim Johnston at *Passages North* ("The Men Who Flew Away"); Aaron Burch at *Hobart After Dark* ("The Professorial Anteater Rises Above & Beyond His Working-Class Background"); Carmen Johnson at Amazon's *Day One* ("The Guava Man"); and Zack Yontz and Kimberly Ann Southwick at *Gigantic Sequins* ("Love Stories").

Thank you to my friends and colleagues at the University of South Carolina: especially Lauren Eyler and Matt Fogarty of the Weirdo Workshop; Elise Blackwell; Kurt Hoberg; and my cohortmates Cayla Fralick, Chris Koslowki, and Rebecca Landau.

Thank you to Diane Boehm, R.S. Deeren, Helen Raica-Klotz, C. Vince Samarco, Pete Stevens, and everyone at

Saginaw Valley State University who helped show me the way.

Thank you to Marlin M. Jenkins, with whom I am always waiting for a train.

Thank you to my family—Mom, Dad, Melissa—who will be happy to know they don't appear in this book at all, not even as anteaters or aliens or elementary school principals.

Thank you to my wife, Lisa, for the best love story I know.

Justin Brouckaert is the author of the hybrid chapbook *SKIN* (Corgi Snorkel Press, 2016). His writing has appeared in *Passages North*, *The Rumpus*, *Catapult*, *DIAGRAM*, *Smokelong Quarterly*, *Prairie Schooner*, and *Bat City Review*, among many other publications. He holds an MFA from the University of South Carolina, where he was a James Dickey Fellow in Fiction. He works in book publishing and lives in Metro Detroit.

A Note on the Text

The body of this text was set in Adobe Carlson Pro designed by William Caslon between 1734 and 1770 and revived by Carol Twombly. The ornamental text was set in VTFLack, created by Adrien Midzic in 2013.

LOVESTORIES&OTHER
LOVESTORIES&OTHER
LOVESTORIES&OTHER
LOVESTORIES&OTHER
LOVESTORIES&OTHER
LOVESTORIES&OTHER
LOVESTORIES&OTHER
LOVESTORIES&OTHER
LOVESTORIES&OTHER
LOVESTORIES&OTHER
LOVESTORIES&OTHER
LOVESTORIES&OTHER
LOVESTORIES&OTHER
LOVESTORIES&OTHER

LOVESTORIES&OTHER
LOVESTORIES&OTHER
LOVESTORIES&OTHER
LOVESTORIES&OTHER
LOVESTORIES&OTHER
LOVESTORIES&OTHER
LOVESTORIES&OTHER
LOVESTORIES&OTHER
LOVESTORIES&OTHER
LOVESTORIES&OTHER
LOVESTORIES&OTHER
LOVESTORIES&OTHER
LOVESTORIES&OTHER
LOVESTORIES&OTHER

9 781950 987115